D0576427

A Beginning-to-Read Book

by Margaret Hillert

Illustrated by Dennis Hockerman

NorwoodHouse Press

DEAR CAREGIVER, The *Beginning-to-Read* series is a carefully written collection of classic readers you may remember from your own childhood. Each book features text comprised of common sight words to provide your child ample practice reading the words that appear most frequently in written text. The many additional details in the pictures enhance the story and offer the opportunity for you to help your child expand oral language and develop comprehension.

Begin by reading the story to your child, followed by letting him or her read familiar words and soon your child will be able to read the story independently. At each step of the way, be sure to praise your reader's efforts to build his or her confidence as an independent reader. Discuss the pictures and encourage your child to make connections between the story and his or her own life. At the end of the story, you will find reading activities and a word list that will help your child practice and strengthen beginning reading skills.

Above all, the most important part of the reading experience is to have fun and enjoy it!

Shannon Cannon

Shannon Cannon,
Literacy Consultant

Norwood House Press • P.O. Box 316598 • Chicago, Illinois 60631
For more information about Norwood House Press please visit our website at *www.norwoodhousepress.com* or call 866-565-2900.

LIBRARY OF CONGRESS CATALOGING-IN-PUBLICATION DATA
Hillert, Margaret.
Tom Thumb / by Margaret Hillert ; illustrated by Dennis Hockerman.– Rev. and expanded library ed.
p. cm.
Summary: Relates a tiny boy's adventure in a cow's mouth, a fish's belly, on the back of a mouse, and at a king's table. Includes reading actvities.
ISBN-13: 978-1-59953-028-4 (library edition : alk. paper)
ISBN-10: 1-59953-028-7 (library edition : alk. paper)
1. Readers (Primary) [1. Readers.] I. Hockerman, Dennis, ill. II. Tom Thumb. English. III. Title.
PE1119.H5833 2006
428.6–dc22 2005033959

We want a little boy.
Little boys are fun.
Where can we get
a little boy?

Oh, look here!
Look in here!
Here is a little boy.
A little, little boy.

Good, good.
This is what I want.
I like this little one.

Mother, Mother.
Look where I am.
Come and get me.
Help! Help!

Oh, my. Oh, my.
How did you get in here?
Come out. Come out.

And get in here.
Now see what you
have to do.

Come with me now.
We will go out here.
We will walk and walk.
Look here.
Here is something big.

Oh, oh.
Here I go.
In, in, in.
Help, Mother! Help!

Here you are.
You are out now.
You are here with me.

I am not with you now.
I am up here.
Up, up, up.

Now here I go down.
Down, down, down.
What can I do?

Oh, help! Help!
Something wants to eat me.
Here I go.

And here I am.
But what is this?
Where am I?

Oh, look. Look.
Here is a little,
little boy.
I want this boy.

Here is something for you.
Sit down on it.
Sit here with me.
I like you.

And I like to ride.
It is fun to ride.
Here is something for
you to ride, too.

This is fun.
I like to do this.
I like to ride and ride.

But I want to go away now.
I want to see my mother and
my father.

Here is something for you.
It is something good to have.
Take it with you.

Oh, this is good.
But it is so big.
It makes me work.
Work, work, work.

Here I am, Mother and Father.
Look what I have.
It is for you.
It will help you.

READING REINFORCEMENT

The following activities support the findings of the National Reading Panel that determined the most effective components for reading instruction are: Phonemic Awareness, Phonics, Vocabulary, Fluency, and Text Comprehension.

Phonemic Awareness: The /th/ sound

Oral Blending: Say the beginning and ending sounds of the following words and ask your child to listen to the sounds and say the whole word:

/th/ + ink = think	/th/ + in = thin	/th/ + umb = thumb
/th/ + ing = thing	/th/ + imble = thimble	/th/ + ick = thick
/th/ + ank = thank	/th/ + ump = thump	/th/ + ird = third

Phonics: The letter Tt

1. Demonstrate how to form the letters **T** and **t** for your child.
2. Have your child practice writing **T** and **t** at least three times each.
3. Ask your child to point to the words in the book that start with the letter **t**.
4. Write down the following words and ask your child to circle the letter **t** in each word:

three	not	the	thumb	kitten	with
father	little	want	with	tap	sit
kite	top	Tom	two	take	this

Vocabulary: Synonyms

1. Write the following words on separate pieces of paper:

little	miniature	tiny	wee	bitty	teeny
huge	gigantic	large	enormous	colossal	immense

2. Read each word to your child and ask your child to repeat it. Explain whether the word means big or small.
3. Fold a sheet of paper in half lengthwise. Draw a line down the middle of the paper. Write the words **small** and **big** at the top each column.
4. Mix the words up. Point to a word and ask your child to read it. Provide clues if your child needs them. Ask your child to place the word in the correct column under the synonym for the word.

Fluency: Choral Reading

1. Reread the story with your child at least two more times while your child tracks the print by running a finger under the words as they are read. Ask your child to read the words he or she knows with you.
2. Reread the story aloud together. Be careful to read at a rate that your child can keep up with.
3. Repeat choral reading and allow your child to be the lead reader and ask him or her to change from a whisper to a loud voice while you follow along and change your voice.

Text Comprehension: Discussion Time

1. Ask your child to retell the sequence of events in the story.
2. To check comprehension, ask your child the following questions:
    - How does Tom Thumb take a bath?
    - What kind of animal gave Tom Thumb a ride?
    - Do you think Tom Thumb was scared of the giant? Why or why not?
    - What things would you like to do if you were as small as Tom Thumb?

WORD LIST

***Tom Thumb* uses the 60 words listed below.**

This list can be used to practice reading the words that appear in the text. You may wish to write the words on index cards and use them to help your child build automatic word recognition. Regular practice with these words will enhance your child's fluency in reading connected text.

a	eat	I	oh	up
am		in	on	
and	father	is	one	walk
are	for	it	out	want (s)
away	fun			we
		like	ride	what
big	get	little		where
boy (s)	go	look	see	will
but	good		sit	with
		makes	so	work
can	have	me	something	
come	help	mother		you
	here	my	take	
do	how		this	
did		not	to	
down		now	too	

ABOUT THE AUTHOR Margaret Hillert has written over 80 books for children who are just learning to read. Her books have been translated into many different languages and over a million children throughout the world have read her books. She first started writing poetry as a child and has continued to write for children and adults throughout her life. A first grade teacher for 34 years, Margaret is now retired from teaching and lives in Michigan where she likes to write, take walks in the morning, and care for her three cats.

Photograph by Glenna Washburn

ABOUT THE ADVISER Shannon Cannon contributed the activities pages that appear in this book. Shannon serves as a literacy consultant and provides staff development to help improve reading instruction. She is a frequent presenter at educational conferences and workshops. Prior to this she worked as an elementary school teacher and as president of a curriculum publishing company.